To Helen and Jamie Cumberbatch - *J.C.*

For my dad and my daughter - *K.W.M.*

Can You Hear
the Sea?

Typeset in Corona medium
Art created with acrylic

Published by Bloomsbury Publishing, New York, London, and Berlin
Distributed to the trade by Holtzbrinck Publishers

Library of Congress Cataloging-in
Publication Data
Cumberbatch, Judy.
Can you hear the sea? / by Judy
Cumberbatch ; illustrated by Ken
Wilson-Max.—1st U.S. ed.
p.   cm.
Summary: Sarah's grandpa gives her
a special shell and says if she listens
carefully she can hear the sea, but all she
hears
are everyday village noises.
ISBN-10: 1-58234-703-4 • ISBN-13: 978-1-58234-703-5
[1. Sound—Fiction. 2. Shells—Fiction.
3. Grandparents—Fiction. 4. Africa, West—
Fiction.] I. Wilson-Max, Ken, ill. II. Title.
PZ7.C9087Can 2006   [E]—dc22   2005053680

First U.S. Edition 2006
Printed in China
10 9 8 7 6 5 4 3 2 1

Bloomsbury Publishing,
Children's Books, U.S.A.
175 Fifth Avenue, New York, NY 10010

Can You Hear the Sea?

by Judy Cumberbatch

illustrated by Ken Wilson-Max

BLOOMSBURY
CHILDREN'S
BOOKS

On Saturday, Sarah's grandpa went into town. Before he left, he gave Sarah a shell. Pink and orange and green, it was the loveliest shell she had ever seen.

"It's a magic shell," said Grandpa. "If you listen carefully, you'll hear the sea."

"Will I really?" asked Sarah.

"Oh, yes," said Grandpa.

On Monday, Sarah listened to her shell by the river as she and Grandma did the washing. But what she heard was . . .

. . . water splashing,

Grandma beating out the sheets,

. . . Reverend Johnson praying,

Kofi playing the drums and singing,

and Grandma humming.

On Sunday, Sarah put
the shell to her ear and
listened on the way
to church. But all she
heard was . . .

"Don't go believing
all that nonsense," said Grandma
as she braided Sarah's hair.

But Sarah didn't listen to her.
Grandpa knew about everything.
He could tell the time by the sun,
knew when the rains would come,
and never, ever told a lie.

and the clothes
flip-flapping in
the wind.

On Tuesday, Sarah and Grandma went to the market. Sarah listened to her shell as she walked between the stalls. But what she heard was . . .

. . . Mr. Victor's sewing machine click-clacking,

Mrs. Nansi's
tongue yak-yakking,

and the market
mammies haggling
all day long.

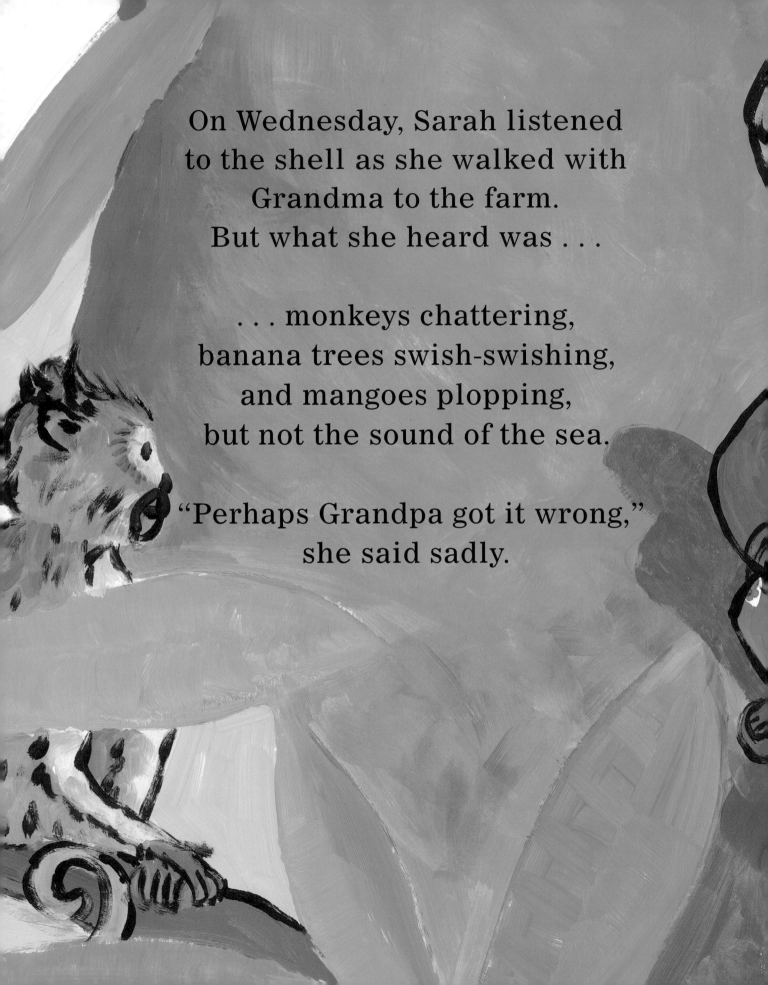

On Wednesday, Sarah listened
to the shell as she walked with
Grandma to the farm.
But what she heard was . . .

. . . monkeys chattering,
banana trees swish-swishing,
and mangoes plopping,
but not the sound of the sea.

"Perhaps Grandpa got it wrong,"
she said sadly.

On Thursday, Grandma turned the whole
house upside down, and Sarah was busy
with the sweeping and the cleaning.
When Sarah listened to the shell
in the evening,
all she heard was . . .

. . . plantains sizzling,
pepper stew
sput-sputtering,
and Grandma snoring.

On Friday, Sarah went to meet Grandpa.
The taxis tooted,
water sellers shouted,
buses hooted,
and Grandpa came.

"That's some silly
shell," she told him.
"I've listened and
listened and heard
everything but the sea."

On Saturday, Grandpa and Sarah sat under the mango tree. Sarah held the shell to her ear.

"Tell me what you hear," Grandpa said.

Sarah listened.

"Boys playing soccer," she said.

"Listen," said Grandpa.

"The next-door neighbor's baby screaming!" cried Sarah. "I can't hear the sea."

"Quiet," said Grandpa. "Now, close your eyes, and this time listen to what the shell tells."

Sarah put the shell to her ear, closed her eyes, and listened. At first, all she could hear was Grandpa's breathing.

Then, as she listened, louder and louder came the sound of water crashing, waves pounding,

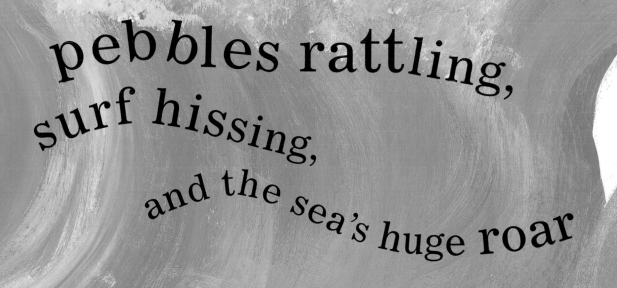

pebbles rattling,
surf hissing,
and the sea's huge roar
on the wide seashore.

"I can hear it," Sarah said.
"I can hear the sea!"

"Didn't I tell you?" said Grandpa, smiling.